Even More Parts

Even More Parts

Even More Parts

Idioms From Head To Toe

Quit messing with my head!

Tedd Arnold

PUFFIN BOOKS

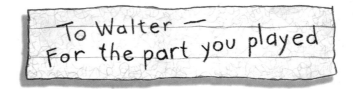

To Walter —
For the part you played

PUFFIN BOOKS
Published by the Penguin Group
Penguin Young Readers Group, 345 Hudson Street, New York, New York 10014, U.S.A.
Penguin Group (Canada), 90 Eglinton Avenue East, Suite 700, Toronto, Ontario, Canada M4P 2Y3
(a division of Pearson Penguin Canada Inc.)
Penguin Books Ltd, 80 Strand, London WC2R 0RL, England
Penguin Ireland, 25 St Stephen's Green, Dublin 2, Ireland
(a division of Penguin Books Ltd)
Penguin Group (Australia), 250 Camberwell Road, Camberwell, Victoria 3124, Australia
(a division of Pearson Australia Group Pty Ltd)
Penguin Books India Pvt Ltd, 11 Community Centre, Panchsheel Park, New Delhi - 110 017, India
Penguin Group (NZ), Cnr Airborne and Rosedale Roads, Albany, Auckland 1310,
New Zealand (a division of Pearson New Zealand Ltd)
Penguin Books (South Africa) (Pty) Ltd, 24 Sturdee Avenue, Rosebank, Johannesburg 2196, South Africa

Registered Offices: Penguin Books Ltd, 80 Strand, London WC2R 0RL, England

First published in the United States of America by Dial Books for Young Readers,
a division of Penguin Young Readers Group, 2004
Published by Puffin Books, a division of Penguin Young Readers Group, 2007

1 3 5 7 9 10 8 6 4 2

THE LIBRARY OF CONGRESS HAS CATALOGED THE DIAL EDITION AS FOLLOWS:
Arnold, Tedd.
Even more parts : idioms from head to toe / Tedd Arnold.
p. cm.
Summary: A young boy is worried about what will happen to his body when he hears such expressions as "I'm tongue-tied,"
"Don't give me any of your lip," and "I put my foot in my mouth."
ISBN 0-8037-2938-3 (hc)
[1. Body, Human—Fiction. 2. Figures of speech—Fiction. 3 Stories in rhyme.] I. Title.
PZ8.3.A647Ev 2004   [E]—dc22   2003056170

Puffin Books ISBN 978-0-14-240714-1
The art was prepared using color pencils and watercolor washes, and the text was hand-lettered by the artist.

Manufactured in China

Sometimes I wish my stupid ears
Weren't always open wide.
They hear such strange and crazy talk—
I'm scared to go outside!

I jotted down a list of all
The scary things I've heard.
Believe me, all of these are real.
I wrote them word for word.

To leave my bedroom unprepared,
I'd have to be a fool!
Excuse me now. There's work to do
Before I go to school.

My eyes are glued to the television.

It cost an arm and a leg.

There are so many **crazy** things
I have to keep in mind!
I sure don't want to accidentally
Leave my parts behind.

Mom says, "Dear, it's time for school.
Let's go or you'll be late."
Then Dad says, "Just remember, son...